13^{72}

Just Like My Dad

Just Like My Dad

by Tricia Gardella

illustrated by Margot Apple

HarperCollins*Publishers*

The illustrations for this book were done on Stonehenge paper with
Holbein oil pastels and lead pencil.

Just Like My Dad
Text copyright © 1993 by Tricia Gardella
Illustrations copyright © 1993 by Margot Apple
Printed in the U.S.A. All rights reserved.
Typography by Elynn Cohen
2   3   4   5   6   7   8   9   10

Library of Congress Cataloging-in-Publication Data
Gardella, Tricia.
   Just like my dad / by Tricia Gardella ; illustrated by Margot Apple.
       p.   cm.
   Summary: A young child glories in the sights, sounds, smells, and
activities of a day spent working on a cattle ranch as a cowhand, just
like Dad.
   ISBN 0-06-021937-8. — ISBN 0-06-021938-6 (lib. bdg.)
   [1. Ranch life—Fiction.   2. Father and child—Fiction.]
   I. Apple, Margot, ill.   II. Title.
PZ7.G164Ju   1993   90-4403
[E]—dc20   CIP
                                                                 AC

With love to my three favorite cowboys:
John Joseph, Sr., John Joseph, Jr.,
and John Joseph, III
—T.G.

To Mother and Dad
and Tante Pauline,
and all my friends
at Stoney B.
—M.A.

When I get up in the morning, I put on my cowboy hat, my chaps . . .

and my spurs . . . just like my dad.

I love the smells of fresh hay
in the barn and leather in the tack shed.

I love the sounds of cows calling softly to their calves and horses munching on their feed in the early morning light. My dad does too.

I love raking the currycomb through my horse Nikki's mane and tail. Nikki likes the soft brush I rub across his back before Dad lifts the saddle onto him.

But I can fasten the cincha and put the bridle on all by myself . . . just like my dad.

Sometimes I can see my breath on crisp autumn mornings.

But my jacket is toasty, and the heat of Nikki's body warms the saddle that creaks beneath my bottom as we move out of the corral.

Often we spend the whole morning mending fence. Dad lets me hammer the staples into the posts.

Soon we are hot, and our jackets are tied behind
our saddles. But work isn't work when I'm with
my dad.

Even lunch is fun, especially when the old-time cowhands start spinning stories about how it was long ago.

Each one of them seems to tell a bigger tale. But
I never get tired of their stories. Neither does my dad.

After lunch we work the herd. I love the noise and the dust and the crowding cattle.

I love the roping and branding.

I love moving the cows from field to field.

Then I like going home, feeling tired but good.
So does my dad.

But the best part of the day is when my dad
tucks me into bed. I never get tired of hearing him
say that one day I will be a great cowhand . . .
just like *his* dad.